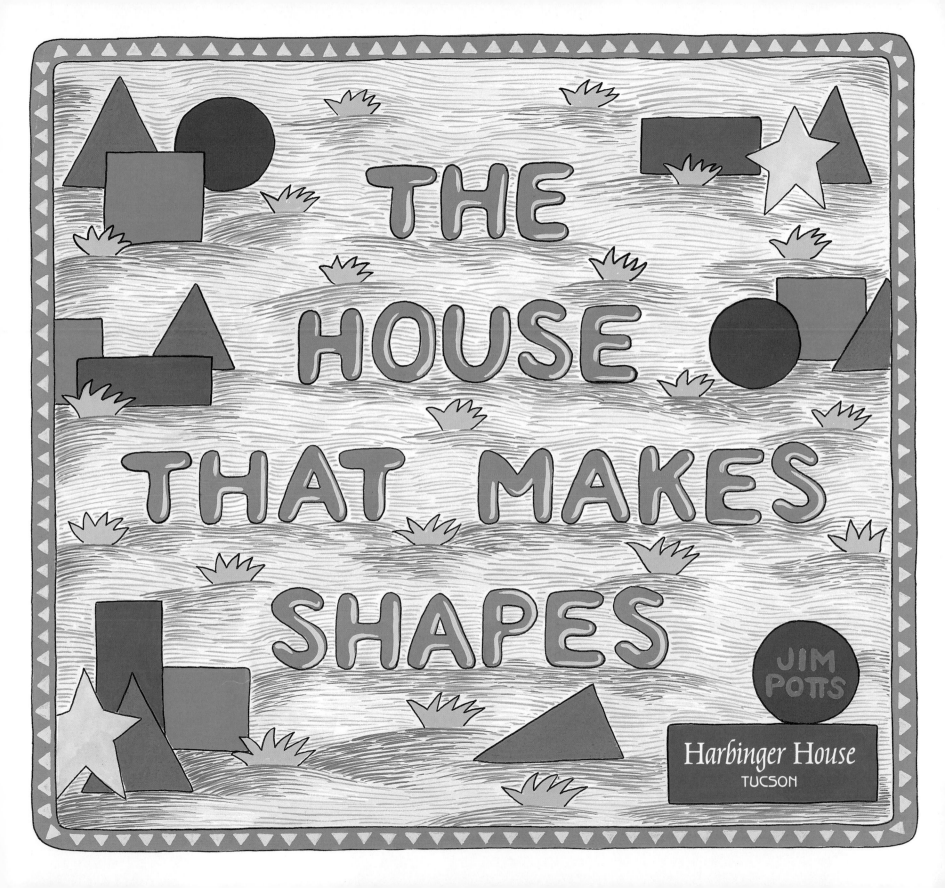

For Mom and Dad, Edelsa
and for Carlos

Thank you Daisy and Carol

HARBINGER HOUSE, INC.
Tucson, Arizona

10 9 8 7 6 5 4 3 2 1

Library of Congress Cataloging-in-Publication Data

Potts, Jim, 1951–
The house that makes shapes / Jim Potts.
p. cm.
Summary: A house shoots shapes out of its roof which a
boy uses to build a house of his own.
ISBN 0-943173-74-4 : $14.95
[1. Shape—Fiction. 2. Dwellings—Fiction.] I. Title.
PZ7.P85754Ho 1992
[E]—dc 20   92-5847

STAR   SQUARE   CIRCLE

THE HOUSE
MADE OF
SHAPES